Note to parents, carers and teachers

Read it yourself is a series of modern stories, favourite characters and traditional tales written in a simple way for children who are learning to read. The books can be read independently or as part of a guided reading session.

Each book is carefully structured to include many high-frequency words vital for first reading. The sentences on each page are supported closely by pictures to help with understanding, and to offer lively details to talk about.

The books are graded into four levels that progressively introduce wider vocabulary and longer stories as a reader's ability and confidence grows.

Ideas for use

- Begin by looking through the book and talking about the pictures. Has your child heard this story before?

- Help your child with any words he does not know, either by helping him to sound them out or supplying them yourself.

- Developing readers can be concentrating so hard on the words that they sometimes don't fully grasp the meaning of what they're reading. Answering the puzzle questions on pages 30 and 31 will help with understanding.

For more information and advice on Read it yourself and book banding, visit www.ladybird.com/readityourself

Book
Band
4

Level 1 is ideal for children who have received some initial reading instruction. Each story is told very simply, using a small number of frequently repeated words.

Special features:

Opening pages introduce key story words

The wheat

Little Red Hen

The rat

The cat

The bread

The dog

The flour

6   7

Careful match between story and pictures

"Will you help me plant the wheat?" asked Little Red Hen.

"No," said the rat, the cat and the dog.

Large, clear type

8   9

Educational Consultant: Geraldine Taylor
Book Banding Consultant: Kate Ruttle

A catalogue record for this book is available from the British Library

Published by Ladybird Books Ltd
80 Strand, London, WC2R 0RL
A Penguin Company

008

ISBN: 978-0-72327-269-4

Printed in China

Little Red Hen

Illustrated by Virginia Allyn

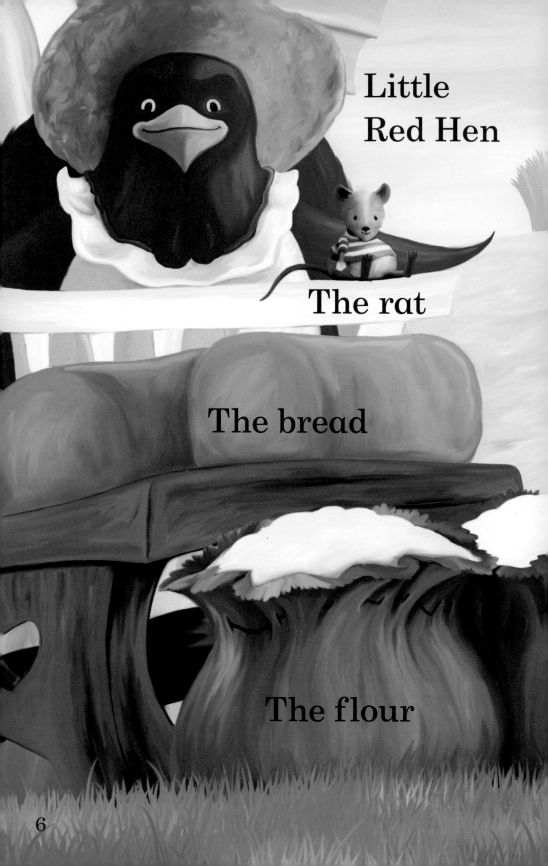

Little
Red Hen

The rat

The bread

The flour

6

The wheat

The cat

The dog

7

"Will you help me
plant the wheat?"
asked Little Red Hen.

"No," said the rat,
the cat and the dog.

9

"Then I will plant
it all by myself,"
said Little Red Hen.

And she did.

11

"Will you help me
cut the wheat?"
asked Little Red Hen.

"No," said the rat,
the cat and the dog.

12

13

"Then I will cut it all by myself," said Little Red Hen.

And she did.

"Will you help me make the flour?" asked Little Red Hen.

"No," said the rat, the cat and the dog.

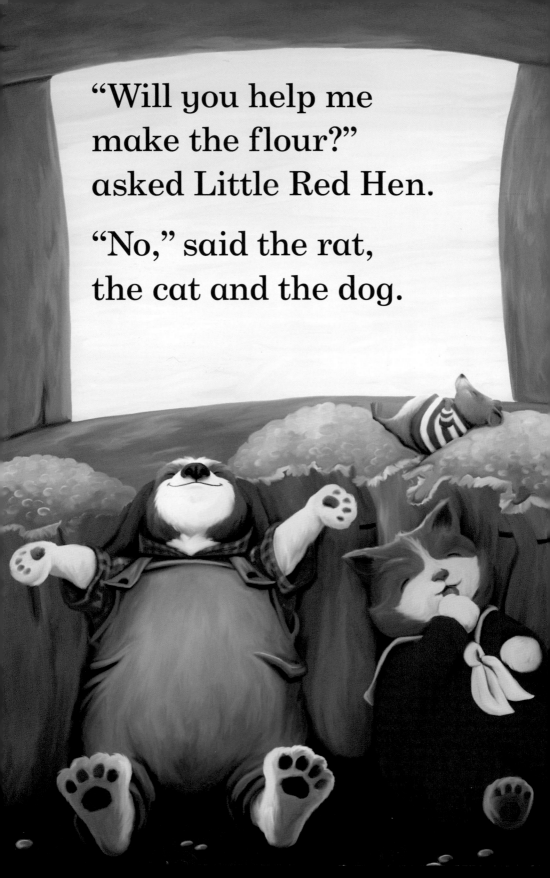

"Then I will make it all by myself," said Little Red Hen.

And she did.

"Will you help me
make the bread?"
asked Little Red Hen.

"No," said the rat,
the cat and the dog.

"Then I will make it all by myself," said Little Red Hen.

And she did.

"Will you help me
eat the bread?"
asked Little Red Hen.

"Yes," said the rat,
the cat and the dog.

27

"No," said Little Red Hen.
"I will eat it all by myself."

And she did!

How much do you remember about the story of Little Red Hen? Answer these questions and find out!

- Who does Little Red Hen ask to help her?

- What do they do instead of helping her?

- What does Little Red Hen eat all by herself?

Look at the pictures from the story and say the order they should go in.

A

B

C

D

Read it yourself with Ladybird

Tick the books you've read!

Level 1
For children who are ready to take their first steps in reading.

- The Enormous Turnip
- Fairy Friends
- Goldilocks and the Three Bears
- Little Red Hen
- The Magic Porridge Pot
- Little Creatures
- Recycling Fun!
- The Princess and the Pea
- Cinderella
- Rex the Big Dinosaur
- The Tale of Peter Rabbit
- The Three Billy Goats Gruff
- Why Giraffe has a Long Neck
- Topsy and Tim Go to the Zoo
- The Ugly Duckling
- The Emperor's New Clothes

Level 2
For beginner readers who can read short, simple sentences with help.

- Beauty and the Beast
- Chicken Licken
- Little Red Riding Hood
- Nature Trail
- Sports Day
- Pirate School
- Rumpelstiltskin
- Sleeping Beauty
- The Gingerbread Man
- Sly Fox and Red Hen
- The Tale of Jemima Puddle-Duck
- The Three Little Pigs
- Why Lion ROARRRS!
- Topsy and Tim The Big Race
- Town Mouse and Country Mouse
- Dom's Dragon

Available on the App Store

The Read it yourself with Ladybird app is now available for iPad, iPhone and iPod touch

App also available on Android devices